Buttercup's
Lovely Day

To my calf.

— CB

To the cows I fed at recess long ago.

— AB

Buttercup's Lovely Day

by Carolyn Beck

illustrated by Andrea Beck

ORCA BOOK PUBLISHERS

I love this day,
the grass at my knees,
the buzz of the bees,
the fluzz of the flies,
switching my tail
and making pies.

I love the clouds
way up high.
They string silly tales
        across the sky:
                downy dogs chase drifty cats,
                        clowny hogs race yaks with hats.

They whiff and waft
and puff around,
dot the sky
and spot the ground,
but never, ever
make a sound.

I love the fields
we ramble and graze,
lazy, languorous,
lingery long days.
I follow the dips
        and jogs
    of the fence,
the roll of the hills,
and a thousand scents.
Crickets sing at the heat.
Hoppers pop at my feet.
I wander, ponder,
eat and eat.

I love my tongue.
It plucks and picks
tender blades
and tasty tips.
I stuff them down
with barely a chew
to Tummy One
where they simmer and stew.
From Tummy One
they go to Two,
then up they come
for a good long chew.

That soggy clod.
My churning jaw.
My cud, my cud
I chomp and chaw.

I love the creek.
It bubbles and guggles
through my legs.
It wraps and pulls
and tugs and begs:
　　　"Buttercup,
　　　　　Buttercup,
　　　　　　　come, my friend,
　　　　　　　　down this way.
　　　　　Let's wind,
　　　let's wend
　　　　away,
　　　　　　away…"
My hooves are set
in the cool wet mud.
I think I'll stay
and chew my cud.
I drink. I chew.
I think. I moo.

I love the bee
that lands on me.
She's fuzzy, she's buzzy
and sweet as can be.
She stamps and stomps
all over my snout.
She's all in a muddle,
can't figure me out.
I am a Buttercup
deep in a patch
of daisies and lilies.
But I don't quite match.
I have a few tassels
and a gorgeous perfume.
But I'm much too big
to be a bloom.
"Moo!" I bellow
so she can see I am me.
Off she flies,
bumbly little bee.

I love the sun
when it sinks down low.
Colors run.
Shadows grow.
       Clump, clump, clump.
             The others go,
       nose to rump,
     full and slow.
Ones and twos,
     bells and moos,
        down the hill,
          around the bend,
       like the creek
     they wind
       and wend.
I watch from my spot
under the tree.
When they're all gone,
there'll be just me.

I love the dark.
It creeps up on me
like the rising tide
of a gentle sea.
A puddle of grey,
a drift of murk,
a hush, a twitch,
a shift, a lurk.
The mossy musk
of the darkening creek.
A bloop!
A swoop!
A flit. A squeak.

I love the critter
who's under my belly.
He's terribly shy
and terrifically smelly.
He whiffs and wafts
and puffs around.
Like a cloud
he makes no sound.
But I dare not think
of what he might do
if I should twitch
or fart
or moo!
I stand very still
till he passes through.
Stinky slinky funky skunk!

I love the night
as it bursts into view,
a star-blasted vast
of deep dark blue.
What is this magic,
this sizzle and twink?
It makes me wonder.
It makes me think.
Is the moon a bucket filled to the top?
Is it brimming with milk?
Did it spill? Did it slop?
Is that milk in the sky?
And here am I, Buttercup, *a cow*.
WOW!! WOW!! WOW!!
It is so, so fine
to be bovine
to be a cow
right here
right now.

I love the man
who comes for me.
He chews on a stem
so thoughtfully.
He lifts his hat
and wipes his brow.
"Buttercup," he says.
"You beautiful cow."
We stand very close
for a good long while.
A nudge, a pat,
a lick, a smile.
Brimming, brimming
with this day, this night,
brimming, brimming,
full and tight.
I say naught, not even a low,
just swing my tail
and turn to go.

I love the path
worn hard and true,
        whisper of grass,
                wet of dew.
    Mice underfoot.
Moon on the rise.
            Drifting mists.
                    Cooling pies.
        Side by side
we wind and wend
            down the hill
and around the bend,
        where a warm light glows
        through a door swung wide,
        and the rustle of cattle
        comes from inside.

I love the barn.
Tree-tall walls.
Cow-filled stalls.
The snorty snuff
of hay and dung.
Pails all stacked,
harnesses hung.
Sweet warm glows
from high-slung lamps.
Bells and lows.
Stomps and stamps.
Bull in his pen
butting his gate.
A horse, a hen,
a cat on a crate.

I love the splat
of milk in a pail,
frothing, splishing,
as I munch from the bale.
When my milk is done,
the light goes dim.
Softly, slyly,
sleep slips in.
My thoughts wind
      and wend
          away,
             away
           to the end,
        to the end
          of a lovely day.

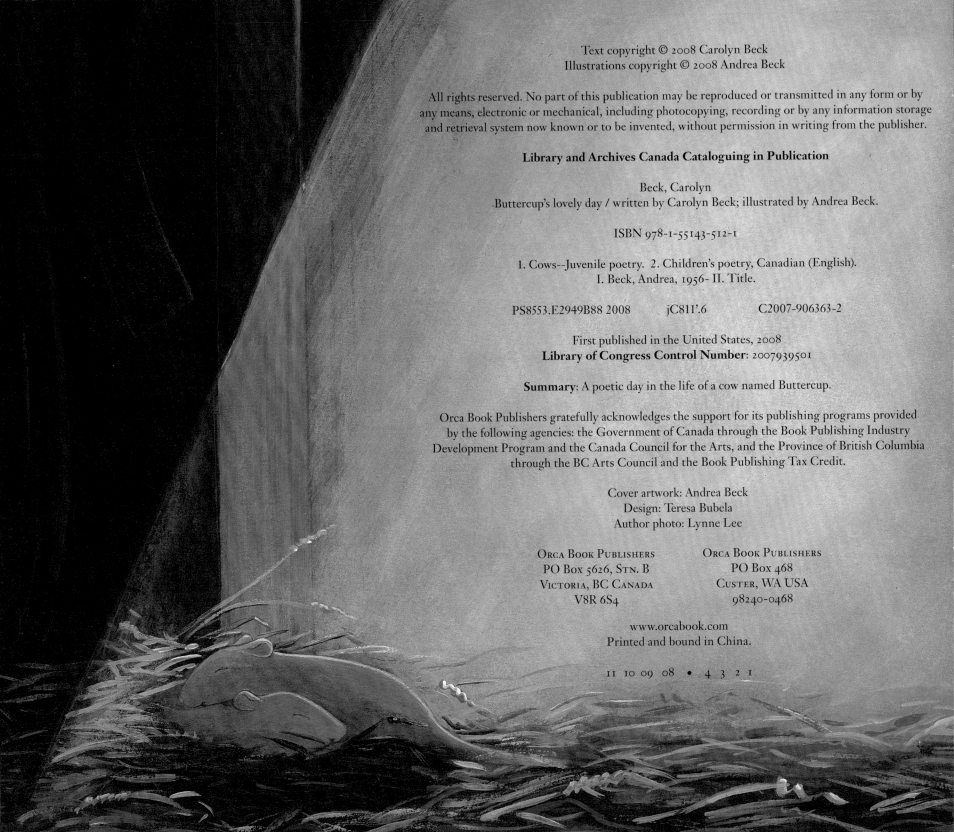

Library and Archives Canada Cataloguing in Publication

Beck, Carolyn
Buttercup's lovely day / written by Carolyn Beck; illustrated by Andrea Beck.

ISBN 978-1-55143-512-1

1. Cows--Juvenile poetry. 2. Children's poetry, Canadian (English).
I. Beck, Andrea, 1956- II. Title.

PS8553.E2949B88 2008   jC811'.6   C2007-906363-2

First published in the United States, 2008
Library of Congress Control Number: 2007939501

Summary: A poetic day in the life of a cow named Buttercup.

Orca Book Publishers gratefully acknowledges the support for its publishing programs provided by the following agencies: the Government of Canada through the Book Publishing Industry Development Program and the Canada Council for the Arts, and the Province of British Columbia through the BC Arts Council and the Book Publishing Tax Credit.

Cover artwork: Andrea Beck
Design: Teresa Bubela
Author photo: Lynne Lee

ORCA BOOK PUBLISHERS
PO Box 5626, STN. B
VICTORIA, BC CANADA
V8R 6S4

ORCA BOOK PUBLISHERS
PO Box 468
CUSTER, WA USA
98240-0468

www.orcabook.com
Printed and bound in China.

11 10 09 08 • 4 3 2 1